English version by Polly Lawson
Illustrations © 1988 Verlag Freies Geistesleben GmbH Stuttgart
English version © Floris Books, 21 Napier Road, Edinburgh, 1988
British Library CIP Data available
ISBN 0-86315-076-4   Printed in West Germany

In Bethlehem long ago

A picture book by Christiane Lesch

Long before Herod became King of the Jews, the prophets had foretold that a saviour would be born from the tribe of David and the people waited with longing for the Son of God who would show them the way to peace.

When the time had come, God sent his angel Gabriel to Nazareth to a maiden called Mary who was going to be married to Joseph of the house of David. The angel came to her and said: "Hail! The Lord God is with you, Mary. He has chosen you from among all woman."

Mary was troubled, but the angel spoke: "Do not fear. You have found grace with God and you will bear a son whom you shall call Jesus."

And Mary asked: "How can that be, seeing I am not yet married to a man?"

The angel answered: "The Holy Spirit will come over you and the child which you will bear will be called God's Son. With God all things are possible. And see, your cousin Elizabeth, the wife of Zechariah, is to have a son despite her old age, because God so wanted it."

And Mary said: "Let the will of God be done."

And the angel went from her.

Soon afterwards, Mary went into the hill country to the house of Zechariah who was a priest of the Temple and she greeted Elizabeth, his wife. And when Elizabeth heard Mary her child leaped in her womb and she spoke, filled with the Holy Spirit: "You are blessed, Mary, for you carry the Son of God under your heart. The mother of our Lord is visiting me! No wonder that my baby is leaping for joy inside me. Children and their children to come will bless you, for you believed the angel."

And Mary said: "My soul praises the Lord and is full of the joy of God, for him I was not too lowly. He has done great things with me. He is mighty and close to those who live in hope."

Mary stayed three months with Elizabeth and then went home.

The time came for Elizabeth's child to be born and she bore a son and after eight days her relations and neighbours came. They wanted to call the child Zechariah after his father. But Elizabeth said: "No, he is to be called John."

They called Zechariah, who had been struck dumb, and told him that his son was to be called John. He asked for a tablet and wrote on it: "He shall be called John."

And from that moment he could speak again and he praised God with a loud voice and all the people heard it with awe and fear. They asked: "What does it mean? And what shall become of this child over whom God holds his hand?"

Zechariah lifted his voice and said: "Child, you shall become a prophet of the Most Holy. You will go before the Lord and prepare his path that he shall guide our feet into the way of peace."

In that time Caesar Augustus ordered that everyone should be taxed and each had to go to his own city. So Joseph who lived as a carpenter in Nazareth, set off with Mary to Bethlehem, the city of David, from which he came. And Mary was with child. When they came to Bethlehem the time had arrived for the child to be born.

They knocked at many doors seeking shelter but nowhere was there room. Too many people had come to Bethlehem.

Finally when they stood before yet another inn which was full, the innkeeper said: "Go into the stable with the ox and the ass. They will keep you warm and there is a roof over your head."

So they found somewhere to stay, and that night Mary gave birth to her first son and wrapped him in swaddling clothes and laid him in the manger.

There were shepherds out in the fields who were watching their flocks by night. And an angel of the Lord came to them, and the Glory of the Lord shone about them, and they were filled with fear. But the angel spoke: "Do not be afraid. I bring you good news of a great joy for all people. For today a Saviour is born who is Christ the Lord. And this shall be a sign. In the city of David you shall find him in a stable wrapped in swaddling clothes and lying in a manger."

And then a multitude of angels appeared to the shepherds. The angels praised God and said: "Glory to God in the highest and on Earth peace to men of good will."

When the angels disappeared the shepherds said to one another:
"Let us go to Bethlehem and find what the angel has told us."
And they went quickly and found Mary and Joseph with a child in
the manger. And they brought their presents and they told about the

angels, and all wondered greatly. But Mary kept these words in her heart.

The shepherds returned to their flock, and they too remembered well what they had seen and heard.

Far in the east a star appeared to the kings Caspar, Melchior and Balthasar. These three kings were wise men who had studied the stars and so they knew that the star meant that a king had been born who would be king over all kings. The star guided them through the desert to Jerusalem. There they asked: "Where is the new-born King of the Jews, who is the Saviour? We have seen his star in the east and have come to worship him."

When Herod heard this he was greatly troubled and all Jerusalem with him.

Herod called the High Priests and the Scribes and asked
them where this king was to be born. And the Scribes told him in
Bethlehem of Judea, as the prophets had written:

"You, O Bethlehem, are by no means least
among the cities of Judah.
There, the Messiah will be born
who will become the Saviour of all mankind."

Herod invited the Wise Men into his palace and asked them about the
star. And he told them to go to Bethlehem and said: "Go and search for
the child there, and when you have found him let me know that I too
may go and worship him."

Caspar, Melchior and Balthasar travelled to Bethlehem and the star went before them. It came to rest over the place where the child was. The three Wise Men were filled with great joy. They went into the house and found the child with his mother. They knelt down, took off the crowns from their heads, and opened the treasures which they had brought. Gold, frankincense and myrrh were their gifts.

When they were going to return to Herod to tell him where to find the child an angel of the Lord warned them in a dream. And the Wise Men understood this and went home by another way.

An angel of the Lord appeared also to Joseph in a dream and warned him: "Arise and flee with the child and his mother to Egypt and stay there until I tell you. For Herod is seeking the child to kill it but he will not succeed."

In the middle of the night Joseph and Mary got up and fled with the child. The ass carried them to Egypt to a safe place.

There they stayed until the time of Herod had passed. And then they returned home to the city of Nazareth.